Dedicated to Mum and Dad

little bee books

An imprint of Bonnier Publishing Group
853 Broadway, New York, NY 10003
Copyright © 2015 by Jo Williamson
First published in Great Britain by Scholastic.
This little bee books edition, 2015.
All rights reserved, including the right of reproduction in whole or in part
in any form. LITTLE BEE BOOKS is a trademark of Bonnier Publishing Group,
and associated colophon is a trademark of Bonnier Publishing Group.
Manufactured in Johor Bahru, Malaysia 02/15
First Edition 2 4 6 8 10 9 7 5 3 1
Library of Congress Control Number: 2015930783
ISBN 978-1-4998-0152-1

www.littlebeebooks.com
www.bonnierpublishing.com

A very big **WOOF** to all you dogs!

Here is my guide to help you have some fun and be happy in your new home...

Just don't tell those **humans!**

The first thing you need to do is choose a human to live with.

They can all look alike...

...but you will know when you have found the right one.

Just like I did.

In your new home, you will realize that you can fall asleep anywhere.

And you will soon...

...find your favorite place.

Remember to always say hello to your human in a friendly way.

And welcome any visitors…

...but be less friendly to strangers.

Your human will want you to be toilet trained...

Mine was very glad when I got the hang of it.

Always be ready for any food that may come along . . .

Your human will be pleased with your help cleaning the floor.

To get extra treats, pretend that you have not been fed.

If that doesn't work...

...you may need to learn some new tricks.

shake   roll   twirl

sing   dance   balance

When playing ball, run straight back and drop it at your human's feet.

If your human gets bored, you could try a different game.

You will meet new neighbors...

...and make lots of friends.

Or sometimes not.

You will find out what you like doing the most...

...and the least.

But you won't really mind as long
as you are with your BEST friend.

And you will be very happy
in your new home.

Just like me.